aMielle-ROSe

A TALE OF FAITH, COURAGE, AND TRIUMPH

BY NICOLE AUSTIN
ILLUSTRATED BY PENNY WEBER

Amielle-Rose: A Tale of Faith, Courage, & Triumph

By Nicole Austin

Auntie Me-Cole & Co.

ISBN 978-1-7351681-7-3

ISBN 978-1-7351681-2-8

ISBN 978-1-7351681-3-5

Written by Nicole Austin

Illustrations: Penny Weber

Art Creative Direction & Interior Design: Linda H. Powers
www.powersdesign.net

Editor: Ann Marie "amc" Collymore

Contributors: My Mommy Gwen

Printed in the United States of America

This book is dedicated to
Trinity and Amari

This book belongs to:

_____

Mustard Seed Faith

Amielle-Rose was a joyful,
shy, and strong little girl.
She was known for her goofy
laugh and beautiful brown hair
that she loved to wear in two large
fluffy puff-balls. She was the happiest when
she spent time with her family traveling and learning new things.
At an early age, Amielle-Rose was introduced to the word faith.
However, she had no clue what it really meant. A few memorable
experiences caused her to learn the true meaning of faith and what
it meant to use it.

Every single night, Amielle-Rose would grab her favorite doll and hop into bed for her nightly routine. Her parents would take turns reading her a Bible story. Some nights her mother would do it, and other nights her father would, but sometimes she was in for a real treat when both her parents would read to her!

Little did she know, reading Bible stories with her parents every night began to teach her about faith. Amielle-Rose enjoyed repeating the stories to her doll and using her own words. This process helped her to see a connection between praying and believing God would answer her prayers. She didn't know how to apply her own faith yet, however, the time would come to experience how strong her faith would actually be.

One day Amielle-Rose and her mother went grocery shopping. While walking down each and every aisle, she began to get bored. Boredom always led to an adventure in her mind! She loved to use her imagination!

As her big hazel eyes became fixed on the bottle of mustard, Amielle-Rose remembered her mother mentioned something the night before called "mustard seed faith" and she was curious as to what it truly meant. Amielle-Rose turned to her mother and asked, "Mom, what exactly does it mean to have mustard seed faith?"

Her mother pulled a pencil from her purse and said, "Sweetheart, do you see how small the lead is on the tip of this sharpened pencil? A mustard seed is about the same size as the tip of this pencil. Small, isn't it?"

Her mother continued, "Well, the Bible talks about mustard seed faith as an example to show people that any ounce of faith, even as small as a mustard seed, is enough to get God's attention. God knew that we would not always be able to see Him, so we would need to believe in Him. We do not make wishes, we say prayers and activate our faith by believing that God will answer those prayers. When times are extremely hard and we find ourselves struggling to use our faith, that is when mustard seed faith comes through for us." Amielle-Rose quietly stared at the pencil.

"Do you know how large a mustard seed can grow?" asked her mother.

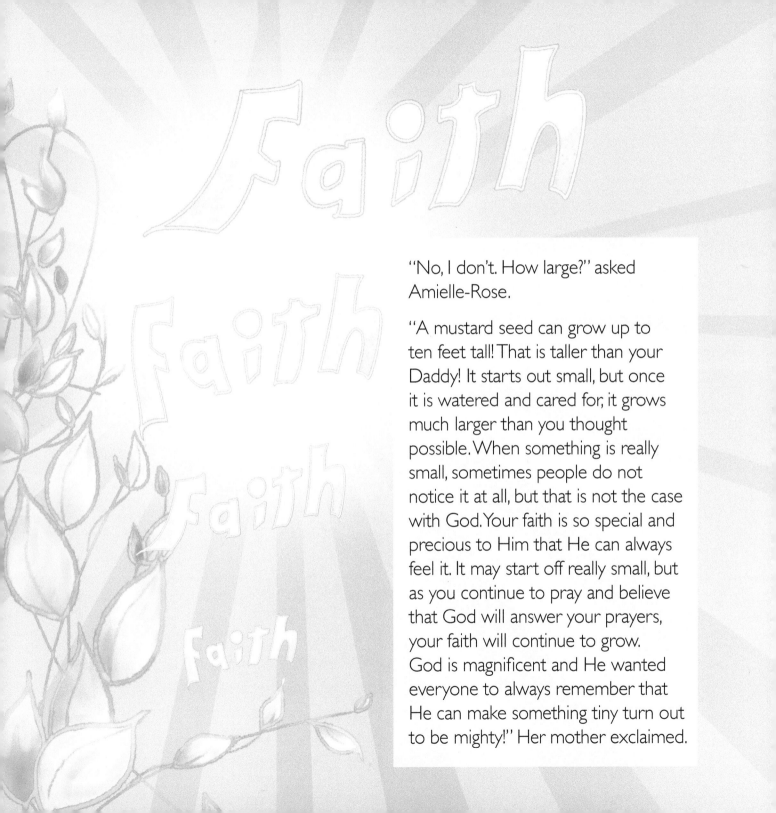

"No, I don't. How large?" asked Amielle-Rose.

"A mustard seed can grow up to ten feet tall! That is taller than your Daddy! It starts out small, but once it is watered and cared for, it grows much larger than you thought possible. When something is really small, sometimes people do not notice it at all, but that is not the case with God. Your faith is so special and precious to Him that He can always feel it. It may start off really small, but as you continue to pray and believe that God will answer your prayers, your faith will continue to grow. God is magnificent and He wanted everyone to always remember that He can make something tiny turn out to be mighty!" Her mother exclaimed.

"Wow! Mustard seed faith sounds powerful! I wonder if it is yellow like mustard. Probably not. I bet it doesn't even have a color. I really want mustard seed faith, but how do I get it? And once I get it, how do I use it?" Amielle-Rose wondered. She had no idea that she would have the chance to find out very, very soon.

The Keys

After a long time in the checkout line, Amielle-Rose and her mother began to walk to the car. Once they arrived at the car, Amielle-Rose walked to the back to help her mother pack the groceries into the back seat. When they were done, her mother closed the back door and walked over to open the front door, but when she pulled the handle nothing happened. Her mother looked over the seat and realized that the keys were in the car. They both began to check every single door for any one of them to be open. No such luck. All the doors were locked!

For a split second, Amielle-Rose grabbed one of her puff balls and began to cry, but then she remembered mustard seed faith. She wondered, "Could God open an unlocked door though? That seems pretty silly, right?" She decided to try anyway and began praying for a door to open so her mom could get inside to get the keys. Amielle-Rose believed that it was possible for God to make that happen. After five minutes of praying, she told her mother to try the door one more time. She closed her eyes, took a deep breath, and listened for the click of the door handle. Click, click! "Praise God!" her mother exclaimed! She ran over and hugged her mom giving her a big squeeze. In that moment, Amielle-Rose understood and believed that God could answer any and every prayer – no matter how big or small. This experience caused her mustard seed faith to grow.

To a child, faith may merely feel like the belief in something – anything! Is that faith? Absolutely not! Amielle-Rose knew that her faith did not come from just anything, it came from God. As her faith continued to increase, she decided to tap into it for another prayer; one that was near and dear to her heart.

The Doll

Christmas was coming and Amielle-Rose still had to give her parents her Christmas list. Her list included small things like bubblegum, lip gloss, video games, and candy. One day, while she was playing dress up in her mom's clothes and makeup, a commercial came on about a Sister-Size Babydoll. The commercial talked about how the doll was the same height as a child, had beautiful hair that can easily be styled, and it came with two sets of matching outfits and accessories for the doll and a child! Amielle-Rose noticed her heart started to beat really fast and she couldn't stop smiling! She imagined herself playing and wearing matching outfits with the doll and became so excited that she started to squeal.

It was official, Amielle-Rose wanted a Sister-Size Babydoll for Christmas. From the very first commercial, she had fallen in love with the doll, and had her heart set on having it as her very own. The Sister-Size Babydoll was special because Amielle-Rose was an only child, so the doll would make her feel like she had a sister. She asked her parents if the doll could be the one and only Christmas gift that she received that year. Amielle-Rose was willing to cancel out all other gifts if it meant that she would get her Sister-Size Babydoll.

"Amielle-Rose never asks for anything. Honey, we really have to get this for her." Amielle-Rose's father said. Her mother looked at him and replied, "You are absolutely right, let's go find the doll."

Her parents searched high and low for the doll but it was sold out EVERYWHERE! Her mother even called her relatives that lived in other states to try and find the doll, but not a single person could find it. Poor Amielle-Rose. This was the one thing she wanted for Christmas and it looked like she would not be getting it. As she sat in her room practicing how to put puff balls in her Sister-Size Babydoll's hair, her parents broke the news to her about the doll being sold out. However, the news did not seem to bother her. As a matter of fact, she told her parents that she already talked to God about it and that her doll would be there for Christmas like she had asked.

Christmas Day arrived and Amielle-Rose ran downstairs to open her gifts. She opened every single gift with anticipation for her beloved doll. The last gift was pretty small, so she knew immediately that it would not be her Sister-Size Babydoll. Amielle-Rose's parents felt absolutely terrible that she had her hopes up to receive the doll on Christmas Day but wouldn't be getting the doll as expected. "Don't worry Amielle-Rose, we will go searching for your doll first thing tomorrow," her mother said. In that moment, Amielle-Rose looked at her parents, giggled, and calmly said, "Christmas Day is not over yet."

Every year on Christmas Day the family gathers together at her Auntie Faye's home to celebrate. As Amielle-Rose and her family arrived, her parents could not help but to watch her and make sure that she was handling everything well. What they hadn't noticed yet was her abundance of faith!

Did they forget that faith can move mountains? Amielle-Rose knew that God would answer her prayer because it meant that much to her. As she sat and ate her favorite holiday pie, she had no idea that God had already set a plan in motion specifically for Amielle-Rose.

"Amielle-Rose!" her Parents exclaimed with excitement. "Come in here!" She immediately ran to the living room to see what her parents were so excited about. She ran so fast that her puff balls blew out of shape!

As she came around the corner, Amielle-Rose saw a large package sitting in the middle of the floor. She jumped up and down three times before she dropped down and started opening the package.

There she was! Her Sister-Size Babydoll, right there staring her in the face.

"I knew it!" She said. "God always comes through! He knew how much I wanted her! He answered my prayer. I learned how to do puff balls so that her hair can look just like mine! I already know her name—Rose!"

Now it is time to hear the backstory. How did the doll get there?

Even though the dolls were sold out everywhere, there happened to be one last doll on hold at a store all the way in Arkansas. Thanks to Amielle-Rose's mom calling every relative she knew asking them to be on the lookout for the doll, her Uncle Jay who lives in the State of Arkansas was able to come across this one last doll. The clerk at the store explained that the doll was on hold. The people who had it reserved had until the end of the day to purchase it. If they didn't return back in time to buy it, it would be available for someone else to take home for a special someone. As the clock ticked, the time had finally come to take the doll off hold. Uncle Jay bought the doll and quickly shipped it to California. He could only remember Uncle Ray's address, so that is where he had it shipped.

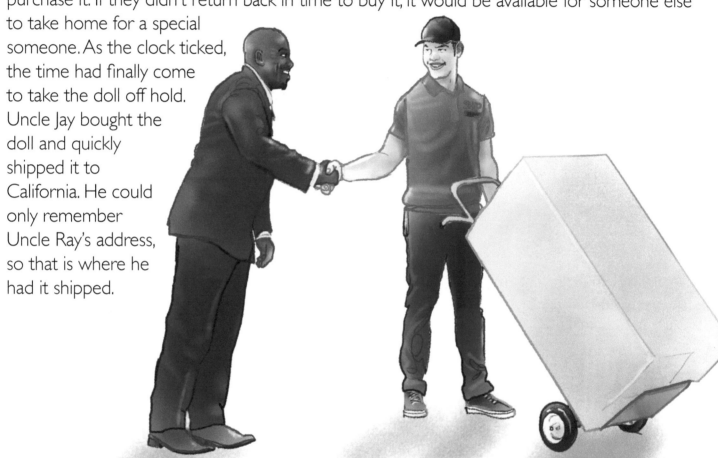

When the doll arrived in California, it looked like it wouldn't be delivered until the day after Christmas because the post office did not deliver on Christmas Day. Amielle-Rose's Uncle Ray and his family were headed down to spend Christmas at Aunt Faye's house as the relatives do every year.

As he and his family were pulling out of their driveway, a post office truck pulled up and blocked them from leaving. The postman got out of the truck and said, "I know we are closed on Christmas Day but something told me to deliver this today." Uncle Ray looked at the package and saw it was addressed to Amielle-Rose, so he put it in the car to bring it to her. He lived about an hour away from Aunt Faye's house; if the postman had arrived a moment too late, these events wouldn't have come to pass. The postman handed the package to Uncle Ray just in time for him to bring it to Amielle-Rose. She kept her faith, and God kept His promise. Amielle-Rose knew that her faith was precious and she needed to nurture and strengthen it as she continued to get older.

The Track Meet

The desire for extra-curricular activities began to flood Amielle-Rose's mind. She knew she wanted to participate in something outside of school, but she just couldn't figure out what to choose. She had a lot of energy that needed to be channeled somewhere. Her mother put her in ballet, jazz dance, and tap dance but Amielle-Rose couldn't find her niche - something that would fit her personality the best. Amielle-Rose spent a large amount of time watching sports with her dad, but nothing fully grabbed her attention.

One day, she saw her mother watching track and field. Something about it spiked her interest! Her mother noticed how intrigued Amielle-Rose would get while watching the sport so she suggested that she should try it out. Amielle-Rose felt her stomach flutter and a sense of excitement began to build up in her chest. She even let out her infamous squeal. Could this be it?

Her mother contacted a local track and field team and scheduled her first tryout. The coach thought she did a great job and invited her to an actual practice with the rest of the team. Her anticipation was so great that she couldn't even sleep the night before her big day.

Amielle-Rose spent the entire morning telling all of her friends about her very first track practice that evening. Hour after hour, the time seemed to move slower and slower. She was so excited, she brought her track clothes to school so she could change as soon as the bell rang.

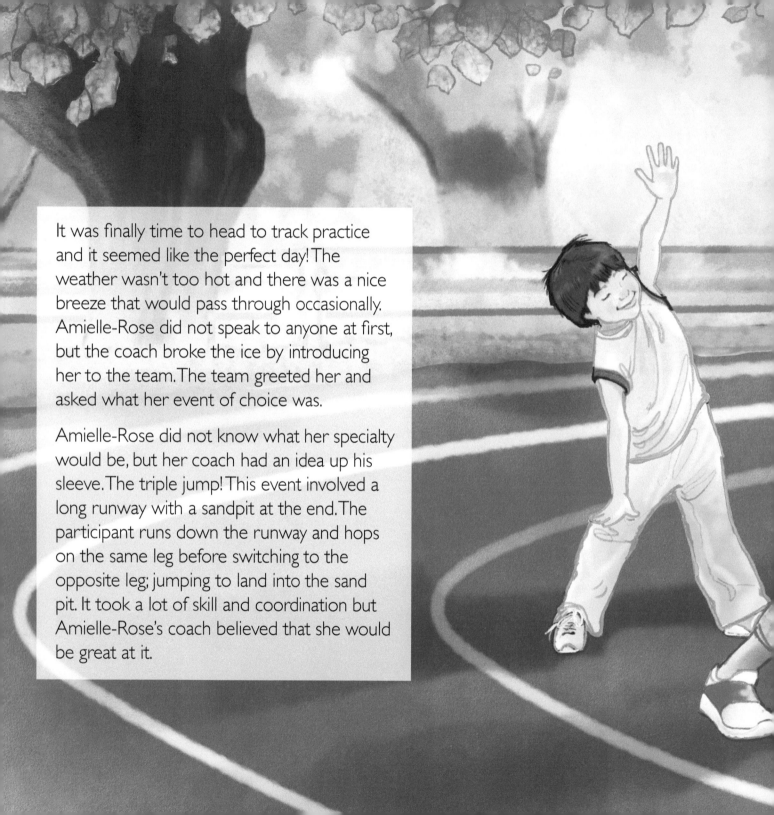

It was finally time to head to track practice and it seemed like the perfect day! The weather wasn't too hot and there was a nice breeze that would pass through occasionally. Amielle-Rose did not speak to anyone at first, but the coach broke the ice by introducing her to the team. The team greeted her and asked what her event of choice was.

Amielle-Rose did not know what her specialty would be, but her coach had an idea up his sleeve. The triple jump! This event involved a long runway with a sandpit at the end. The participant runs down the runway and hops on the same leg before switching to the opposite leg; jumping to land into the sand pit. It took a lot of skill and coordination but Amielle-Rose's coach believed that she would be great at it.

Amielle-Rose enjoyed practicing the triple jump and soon she began to compete in actual track meets. She was still known for her two fluffy puff-balls that people loved to watch as they blew gently in the wind. She had not understood how gifted she was until she qualified for her first major track meets, the National Championships and the Junior Olympics.

You didn't think we forgot about faith do you? Well, we haven't! Faith is on its way to making another appearance.

Amielle-Rose had never participated in an activity that was such a major deal. Once she arrived at the National Championships she became afraid, but she kept it to herself. When warmups began she put on her favorite gospel music and started warming up for the triple jump.

In the triple jump, each contestant is required to take three jumps each. Out of those three, the judges take the top eight jumps and send those participants to the finals. In the finals, each jumper must take three additional jumps. In the end, whoever has the furthest jump out of all six rounds would be named the National Champion.

Amielle-Rose's turn came up and she started running full speed down the runway, but before she knew it, she felt sand under her feet – she had run straight through and didn't jump at all! She realized that her fear had gotten the best of her. With tears beginning to fill her eyes, she looked up into the stands and locked eyes with her sister. Her sister mouthed the words, "You can do all things through Christ…" Amielle-Rose remembered that God had blessed her with the gift to triple jump, just like He blessed her with her doll. She began to pray and ask God to help her relax and just have fun.

I can do all things through Christ who strehgthens me

Hop, step, jump… silence… 36 feet 11 inches!

Amielle-Rose moved into the lead and officially became the new national champion!

It almost felt like a dream.

She could not believe she had won such a huge track meet! As she took her stand at the top of the podium, she fluffed her puff-balls as feelings of pure joy began to flood her heart. She felt butterflies in her stomach and immediately began to thank God for her gift and allowing her to experience such an incredible feat.

Every year the track team that Amielle-Rose belonged to would host their own track meet. Once she arrived, she noticed a lot of people looking at her and it was more than just a glance, there were stares!

"What's going on? Why are these people staring at me like this?" she thought to herself. Just as the idea of curling up into a ball to hide started to arise, her friend Erin walked up to her and showed her an event program. Amielle-Rose opened the program and her heart sank into her stomach.

On the seventh page of the book there was a picture of Amielle-Rose and a full article stating she would break the national record in the triple jump on that same day. She became so nervous she even wanted to change her signature puff-ball hairstyle so no one would notice her. She ran to the restroom to calm herself down. Amielle-Rose could not believe her coach had put that article in the program for everyone to see. What if she didn't break the record? What then? What would people think if she couldn't do it?

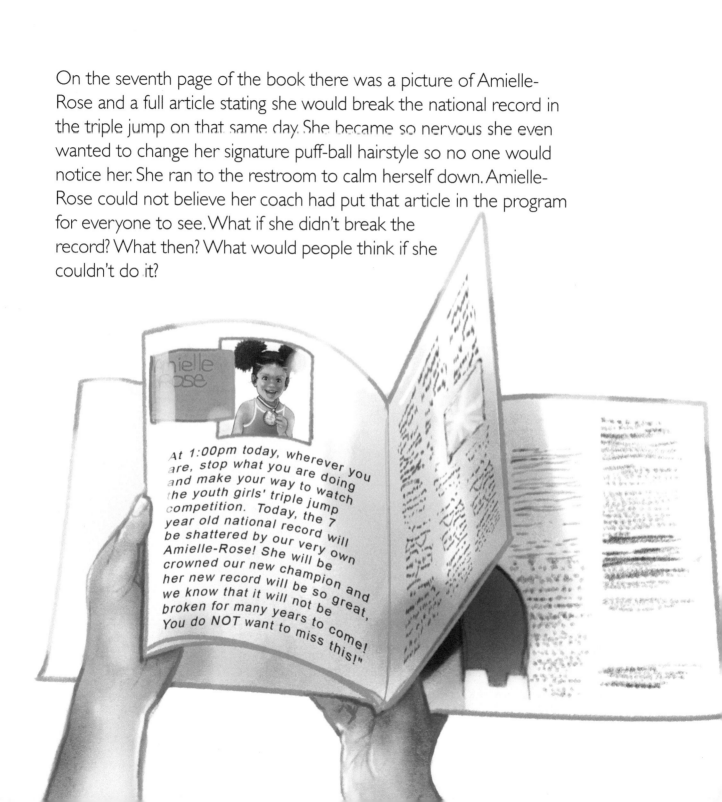

At 1:00pm today, wherever you are, stop what you are doing and make your way to watch the youth girls' triple jump competition. Today, the 7 year old national record will be shattered by our very own Amielle-Rose! She will be crowned our new champion and her new record will be so great, we know that it will not be broken for many years to come! You do NOT want to miss this!"

As Amielle-Rose's emotions began to overtake her, one of her favorite gospel songs started playing on her phone. She started tapping her fingers and singing along until she began to feel at ease and decided to pray. "Lord, I know you have blessed me with an incredible gift. If you feel it's okay, please help me break the national record today so I can make my family and friends proud." Before long, it was time to begin warming up.

As she walked out onto the competition field, she noticed a lot of people had gathered near the triple jump competition pit. Amielle-Rose began to whisper her favorite Bible verse - Philippians 4:13, "I can do all things through Christ who strengthens me." Repeating this allowed her to calm down and be at peace. When it was her turn to jump she took a deep breath and said, "Ok Lord, it's just me and You." She took off running down the runway. She felt very light, powerful, and fast.

Her excitement was cut short, however, when a person abruptly raked the pit.

"NO! NO! NO! You are not supposed to rake the pit until all of the track officials come over, take a picture, and verify the record first!"

Due to the fact that it was raked too quickly, they were not able to make it official and Amielle-Rose was asked to do it again. She became so angry and frustrated that it began to distract her. Her next jump did not break the record. She was upset and overwhelmed. She needed to take a moment, so she did.

"Lord, I am so sorry I let this get in the way of what you have blessed me to do already. You allowed me to break the record once today, I believe you can allow me to do it again." She took a deep breath and got ready to jump one more time.

Hop… step… jump… 39 feet 1.5 inches! It was a
new national record! Amielle-Rose was shocked and
in disbelief but she also felt very gracious and humble.

As the officials came over to note
the new record for the record
book, Amielle-Rose calmly sat
down and took it all in.

Once everything was over she went to sit with her friends, but she did not say a word. She sat quietly to thank God and ask Him to show her how she can express her true appreciation for the blessings He had given her. Something had sparked in her. Amielle-Rose saw how powerful faith can be. She understood that God can answer any prayer, no matter how big or small, as long as she did her part and had faith. Faith had become a part of who she was. It was in her blood now, flowing through her veins! God had blessed Amielle-Rose with the gift of undeniable faith and she chose to exercise it every chance she could. Not only did she love to activate her faith, but she also loved to encourage others to do the same in their time of need.

Amielle-Rose began to tell her story of faith to anyone that would listen, especially young people. She felt that being young does not mean that their faith would not be as powerful as an adult's. She understood that God gives all of us a measure of faith. Once she activated her own, she never looked back!

Are you ready to activate yours?